This Faber book
belongs to:

_ _ _ _ _ _ _

'I love MaCATity.' (Me – It's Macavity.)
'Yes that's what I said, MaCATity, because he looks like my cat and he is a very very funny naughty naughty cheat. And my name is on the cover (Arthur Robins).'

Robin, age 4, and mum, Donna

'This was fun to read to my little sister. I read the story and she shouted "Macavity's not there!" a lot and in her loudest voice.'

Hal, age 11

'We loved this book! We read it once, then Hazel asked me again the next day to read the story about the cat "they can't find".'

Hazel, age 4, and mum, Shona

'I like the funny police dog and the naughty cat!' Otto, age 6

'All the cats are naughty, aren't they – but Macavity is the naughtiest.'

Seb, age 4

For all the cats I have known:
Bugsy, Tootsie, Beryl, Tiggle, Mittens, Benjy, Nugget, Patsy, Ollie, Versace and Mrs Grumpy. A. R.

From the original collection, 'respectfully dedicated to those friends who have assisted its composition by their encouragement, criticism and suggestions: and in particular to Mr. T. E. Faber, Miss Alison Tandy, Miss Susan Wolcott, Miss Susanna Morley, and the Man in White Spats. O. P.'

First published in 1939 in *Old Possum's Book of Practical Cats*
by Faber and Faber Ltd,
Bloomsbury House, 74—77 Great Russell Street, London WC1B 3DA
This edition first published in 2014

Printed in China

Illustrations © Arthur Robins, 2014
Design by Ness Wood

A CIP record for this book is available from the British Library

HB ISBN 978—0—571—31212—2
PB ISBN 978—0—571—30813—2

10 9 8 7 6 5 4 3 2 1

FSC
MIX
Paper from responsible sources
FSC® C008047
www.fsc.org

➤ A FABER PICTURE BOOK ◄

Macavity

Written by T. S. Eliot

Illustrated by
Arthur Robins

ff

FABER & FABER

Macavity's a Mystery Cat:

he's called the
Hidden Paw—

For he's the master criminal
who can defy the law.

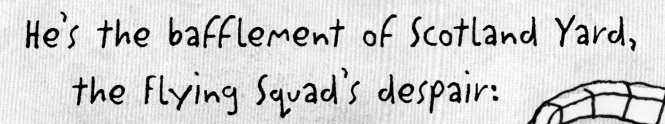

He's the bafflement of Scotland Yard,
the Flying Squad's despair:

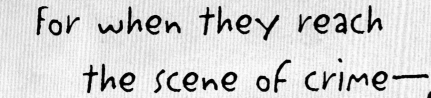

For when they reach
the scene of crime—

Macavity's not there!

Macavity, Macavity,
there's no one like Macavity,

He's broken every human law,
he breaks the law of gravity.
His powers of levitation would
make a fakir stare,

And when you reach the
scene of crime—

Macavity's not there!

Macavity's not there!

Macavity's a ginger cat,
he's very tall and thin;

You would know him if you saw him,
for his eyes are sunken in.

His brow is deeply lined with thought,
his head is highly domed;

His coat is dusty from neglect,
his whiskers are uncombed.

He sways his head from side to side,
 with movements like a snake;
And when you think he's half asleep,
 he's always . . .

wide awake.

Macavity, Macavity,
    there's no one like Macavity,
for he's a fiend in feline shape,
    a monster of depravity.

You may meet him in a by-street,
   you may see him in the square—

SQUARE

But when a crime's discovered, then

Macavity's not there!

He's outwardly respectable.
   (They say he cheats at cards.)
And his footprints are not found in
   any file of Scotland Yard's.

And when the larder's looted,
  or the jewel-case is rifled,
Or when the milk is missing,
  or another Peke's been stifled,
Or the greenhouse glass is broken,
  and the trellis past repair—

Ay, there's the
wonder of the thing!

Macavity's
not there!

And when the Foreign Office find
   a Treaty's gone astray,
Or the Admiralty lose some plans
   and drawings by the way,

There may be a scrap of paper in the
   hall or on the stair—
But it's useless
   to investigate—

Macavity's not there!

And when the loss has been disclosed,
the Secret Service say:

It MUST have
been Macavity!

—but he's a mile away.
You'll be sure to find him resting,
or a-licking of his thumbs,

Or engaged in doing complicated long division sums.

Macavity, Macavity, there's no one like Macavity,
There never was a Cat of such
    deceitfulness and suavity.

He always has an alibi,
    and one or two to spare:
At whatever time the
    deed took place—

MACAVITY WASN'T THERE!

And they say that all
the Cats whose wicked
deeds are widely known

(I might mention Mungojerrie,

I might mention Griddlebone)

Are nothing more than agents
for the Cat who all the time
Just controls their operations:

the Napoleon of Crime!